Andi to the Rescue

Circle C Stepping Stones

Circle C Stepping Stones #4

Andi to the Rescue

Susan K. Marlow

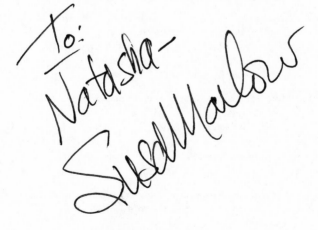

To:
Natasha —

Susan Marlow

Kregel
Publications

Andi to the Rescue
© 2017 by Susan K. Marlow

Illustrations © 2017 by Leslie Gammelgaard

Published by Kregel Publications, a division of Kregel, Inc., 2450 Oak Industrial Dr. NE, Grand Rapids, MI 49505.

ISBN 978-0-8254-4433-3

Printed in the United States of America
17 18 19 20 21 22 23 24 25 26 / 5 4 3 2 1

Contents

New Words

aggie—a marble made from a certain type of stone called agate

carriage house—a garage-like place to keep buggies and carriages

dawdle—to move slowly and waste time

jefe—(HEF-ay) the Spanish word for "boss"

kindling—small pieces of wood that catch fire easily

lean-to—a small shed or shelter with three walls and a slanting roof

loot—stolen goods

mischievous—naughty; not well-behaved

obliged—grateful; to owe someone a favor

pneumonia—a life-threatening illness that attacks a person's lungs

poncho—a large blanket or waterproof cloth with a slit in the middle for a person's head to go through

privy—an outside toilet; an outhouse

ransom—to demand money to return captives to their family

souvenir—a reminder of an event; a keepsake

venison—deer meat

⇥ CHAPTER 1 ⇤

Poor Miss Hall

Late Fall 1877

Nine-year-old Andi Carter clomped down the school-house stairs. Recess at last! She looked up into the dreary November sky.

Plop! A raindrop landed on her cheek. "Rain, rain, go away," Andi shouted at the dark clouds.

Andi's friend Cory Blake took the porch steps in one leap and landed next to Andi. "Come again another day!" he finished. He tipped his head back and stuck out his tongue to try to catch a drop.

Cory clearly didn't care if the rain stayed or came another day. Or even if it poured buckets. He looked glad to be out of the classroom for twenty minutes.

Recess was definitely the best part of the school day.

Cory looked at Andi and jiggled his pocket. Marbles clicked. "Did you bring back my special aggies?"

"I forgot."

Cory slumped. "You said you'd let me try and win 'em back today."

"I'll bring them tomorrow," Andi promised.

A stiff breeze whipped her face. She buttoned her coat and jammed her wool hat farther down on her head. "Besides, it's too cold to sit on the ground and play marbles. I'm gonna jump rope."

She skipped away and joined a group of little girls. Two were twirling the long rope. The rest stood waiting their turns. Andi hopped on one foot and then on the other to keep warm.

More raindrops splashed on her sleeves.

When Andi's turn came, she jumped as fast as the rope slapped the ground. After fifteen jumps, she warmed up enough to tear off her hat. Two long, dark braids bounced against her back.

". . . thirty-one, thirty-two," the girls chanted.

Andi panted and kept jumping. Mary Ellen Meyers had made it all the way to fifty-seven jumps, and Andi was determined to beat her.

A loud scream broke Andi's concentration. The girls dropped the rope.

"Hey!" Andi shouted. The rope lay limply at her feet. "That doesn't count."

Nobody listened to her. Mary Ellen gasped. "Oh, my goodness!"

Andi whirled. Next to the seesaw, Julianna Ross lay sprawled on the ground, screaming. Never mind that she didn't look hurt from her fall. Her disgrace was ten times worse. Every pupil in the schoolyard was staring at her.

Julianna sat up. She looked at her mud-splattered coat and hands and let out another ear-piercing shriek.

Miss Hall came barreling out of the schoolhouse like a mama cow looking for her calf. "Whatever is the matter?" She started down the stairs.

After the teacher's first step, everything happened too fast for Andi to remember all the details. Miss Hall's long skirt might have caught on a nail. Perhaps she took the steps too fast. Or maybe the rain had turned the stairs slippery.

Whatever the reason, Miss Hall went down hard. There were only six steps, but it must have felt like twice that many to the aging schoolteacher. When she finally tumbled to a stop at the bottom, she hit her head and lay still.

Mary Ellen and three others screamed. Boys and girls swarmed around Miss Hall. Some cried, but most stood stock-still in horror.

Julianna stopped shrieking and ran over to see what had happened.

"Is she d-dead?" Cory stuttered. His freckles stood out against his pale cheeks.

Andi let out the breath she'd been holding. Cory sure was brave to ask that question.

"Don't be a goose," Sarah Jones scolded. She crouched beside Miss Hall's still form. "Of course she's not dead."

At almost fifteen years old, Sarah along with Andi's sister Melinda were the oldest girls in the school.

Andi winced. Correction. Only Sarah was the oldest girl now. Melinda had gone to San Francisco to study at a young ladies' academy for the year.

I wish Melinda was here! Andi wanted her big sister to put her arms around her and tell her Miss Hall would be all right.

Thomas, the oldest boy, joined Sarah beside the still form. "All of you hush!" he ordered. The children quieted. "Miss Hall?" He gently shook her shoulder. "Are you all right, ma'am?"

A low moan greeted the small crowd.

"Move back." Thomas shooed everyone away. "You'll smother her."

Andi and the rest of the children jumped back to give Miss Hall more air. None of the younger pupils ever disobeyed fifteen-year-old Thomas—not even mean Johnny Wilson, the classroom bully.

Miss Hall moaned again.

From a safe distance, Andi watched Thomas and Sarah help the teacher up.

When Miss Hall tried to stand, she cried out and crumpled back to the ground. "I'm sorry, children," she whispered. "I fear I have twisted my ankle."

Andi bit her lip and glanced at her friends. They looked as frightened as Andi felt. Miss Hall couldn't be hurt. What would happen now? Who would teach their class if—

Sarah shook Andi's shoulder. "Stop woolgathering and do what I told you."

"Huh?" Andi pulled her bewildered gaze from Miss Hall. "What?"

"Run and get your brother," Sarah said. "He's on the school board. He'll know what to do."

Happy to be given a task, Andi bolted out of the schoolyard and ran the four blocks to her oldest brother's law office. She slammed through the door. *"Justin!"*

His office looked deserted. Maybe Justin was across the street at the courthouse, presenting an important case.

Andi's heart sank. She knew better than to barge into a courtroom uninvited. Judge Morrison would peer over his spectacles and scold her in his courtroom voice. He might even bang his gavel, which would embarrass Justin and frighten Andi.

No, she couldn't go looking for Justin. *What do I do now?*

Just then the door to a small, private office opened. Justin appeared in the doorway. "What's the matter, Andi?" He crossed the room. "Why aren't you in school?"

A big lump clogged Andi's throat. No words came out.

Justin led Andi into his office and set her on his desktop. "Big breath, honey. What's wrong?"

Andi took a big breath, which helped a little. She swallowed the lump. "It's Miss Hall."

"What happened to her?"

Tears filled Andi's eyes. Her cheeks felt hot and flushed from running. Her heart raced. "She fell down the stairs and can't get up. Sarah sent me to get you."

Justin pulled a handkerchief from his vest pocket and dabbed Andi's eyes. "And so you have. Let's go see." He helped her down from the desk, found his hat, and put it on. "I'm sure it's not as bad as it sounds."

Andi slumped. She couldn't run all the way back to school just yet. "Will you carry me?"

"You're too big to carry."

"But—"

"Luckily, Thunder is tied up just outside." Justin winked.

Yippee! Andi's tears dried up in a hurry.

Justin climbed into Thunder's saddle and pulled

Andi in front of him. With a touch of Justin's heels, the big, bay horse trotted down the street.

A horseback ride during the school day was an unexpected delight. Andi sat up straight and tall, all smiles. *Too bad the schoolhouse isn't clear across town.*

Two short minutes later, Justin pulled Thunder to a stop in the schoolyard. He lowered Andi to the ground and dismounted.

Miss Hall sat on the bottom step. Her face was still pale, and her bun had come undone. Strands of gray-streaked brown hair fell about her shoulders. A bruise was beginning to darken her forehead.

She gave Justin a weak smile. "Thank you for coming, Justin. I'm afraid I was a bit clumsy this morning. Thomas went for the doctor."

Justin scooped Miss Hall up in his arms as if she weighed no more than Andi. "I'll take you home. You can freshen up before you see the doctor."

Color returned to the teacher's cheeks. She smiled. "You always were my favorite pupil."

"School is dismissed," Justin announced. "You older pupils see that the younger ones get home. Andi, bring Thunder and follow me."

Andi jumped to obey. *No more school today!*

⊰ CHAPTER 2 ⊱

Sick?

It was too bad Miss Hall had fallen and sprained her ankle. Andi felt sorry for her teacher. But she didn't feel sorry that school had closed for the rest of the week. The school board wanted to meet and decide what to do with twenty-five pupils who now had no teacher.

Andi wriggled with joy. Three whole days without school. Three extra days to ride Taffy, her palomino filly.

The rain washed away Andi's horse-and-rider plans the very next morning. Worse, it poured the rest of the week. Instead of galloping Taffy up to her special spot, Andi spent every afternoon in her filly's stall, curled up under a blanket with one of her brother Mitch's dime novels.

Andi wished she could read this exciting story to

Sadie, just like her friend Riley used to do for Andi when she couldn't read. Riley had left the ranch months ago, and it was too cold and too wet to ride out to Sadie's sheep ranch.

She read the dime novel to Taffy, but it wasn't the same.

In spite of the weather, Andi stayed cheerful the rest of that whole rainy week.

"Maybe school will stay closed until Miss Hall's ankle heals," she whispered in Taffy's ear. "It can't rain forever. Soon as it lets up, we'll go for a ride."

But the rain did not let up. Worse, school did not stay closed.

"Your holiday is over," Justin told Andi at supper Saturday night. "We found someone to take over the classroom until Miss Hall is better."

"Who?"

Justin smiled and winked, like he was giving her the best news ever. "Mother."

Mother? Her big brother must be teasing.

"Finish your supper, Andrea," Mother said calmly. She did not seem to be in on any joke.

Andi's stomach turned over. What would the other kids say when they found out Mother was taking Miss Hall's place?

I can't go to school on Monday. I just can't.

"Watch out, little sister!"

Andi jumped back from the cookstove. Why did Chad always sneak up on her?

Chad poured himself a cup of coffee from the shiny brass pot. "Hurry up," he called as he pushed through the swinging door into the dining room. "Breakfast is getting cold."

As soon as Chad disappeared, Andi crept closer to the stove again. She pulled back her long, dark hair so it wouldn't catch fire. Then she leaned her face close to the hot metal.

"One, two, three . . ." She counted the seconds. *Can I make it all the way to—*

"Ouch!" Andi stepped away and felt her burning face. She could tell without looking in the mirror that her cheeks glowed a nice, rosy red. "This has got to work. It just has to."

She coughed and sniffled. She tried to sneeze, but she couldn't make one come out.

Andi pushed open the door and dragged her feet to where Mother sat at one end of the breakfast table. Justin sat at the other end. Chad and Mitch sat on one long side.

Melinda's chair was empty. It would stay empty all this school year except for a short visit during the Christmas holidays.

Andi wrinkled her nose. She could not think of one good reason why Melinda would want to leave her family, the ranch, and her horse to spend a whole year in the city.

Especially if it meant staying with grumpy old Aunt Rebecca.

When Andi watched Melinda board the train in September, she decided that older sisters must be a little bit crazy. But Mother said Melinda liked the city. She liked going to a young ladies' academy. She enjoyed meeting people, making new friends, and seeing the sights.

Not Andi. She liked staying on the ranch with Taffy. She'd rather work on her lassoing skills than learn a new embroidery stitch or a fancy dance step.

"Stop daydreaming and find your seat, Andrea," Mother said. "We're waiting on you so Justin can ask the blessing."

Andi covered her mouth as a big cough burst from her throat. She tried to make it sound deep and harsh. "Feel my cheeks," she croaked. "I must have a fever."

Mother laid the back of her hand against Andi's forehead.

"No, Mother. Feel my *cheeks*."

Chad grinned. "So that's why you hung back in the kitchen for so long."

Shhh! Andi glared at him.

"You're not sick, sweetheart." Mother smiled. "Surely you're not trying to find a way to stay home just because I'm going to be your teacher? It's only until the holidays. Miss Hall will return after the New Year."

Andi sighed. So much for her great idea. "No, ma'am. I guess not."

Mother hugged Andi and sent her to her seat. Justin prayed for their meal. Soon, everybody was eating breakfast.

Chad sawed away at his ham and looked at Andi. *Glad it's you and not me*, his twinkling blue eyes said. He chuckled and popped a big piece of meat in his mouth.

Thank goodness it kept him from saying anything out loud.

"Chad." Mother didn't need to say anything more. Her gaze bored into Chad like a hot branding iron on a calf.

Chad got the message. He dug into his biscuits and gravy and kept his chuckles inside.

Andi ate half a biscuit and most of her ham. She swallowed her milk in four big gulps and asked to be excused.

"Yes, you may," Mother said, rising from the table. "Don't dawdle. Wash up. Then find your books and your coat. Don't forget your hat. The rain's coming down in rivers this morning."

"Yes'm."

"When you're finished, hurry out to the front yard.

Mitch will have the buggy hitched up by the time you get there."

Justin winked at Andi when she passed him on her way out of the dining room. "Cheer up, honey. You'll have a fine day. I promise."

Andi did not smile at her favorite brother. Not even a wink would help her get through this day.

She washed up at the kitchen pump and ran up the back stairs. *No dawdling!*

She yanked her red wool coat from the wardrobe and dug around for her hat. Then she scooped up her books and darted down the hallway.

Andi paused when she reached the top of the wide staircase. Twenty steps curved down from the upstairs hallway to the entryway near the front door.

Andi peeked to the right. The polished wood banister was too tempting to resist.

She peeked to the left. Their housekeeper Luisa was nowhere in sight. Mother never scolded Andi for sliding down the railing, but Luisa scolded her every time—in Spanish.

Before she changed her mind, Andi hiked up her coat and dress. She clutched her books under one arm, climbed aboard, and pushed herself backward.

Whee! Andi sailed down the banister. Her hat came off. Schoolbooks fell to the floor.

She gripped tighter. Her palms screeched against

the smooth wood, but she didn't slow down. She glanced behind her shoulder—

Whoosh! Andi flew off the banister straight into Justin's arms.

Smack! They hit the floor together.

Quick as a bucking bronco, Andi leaped up. Her hands flew to her cheeks. "I'm sorry!"

Justin lay groaning on the hardwood floor.

"Are you all right?" Andi asked.

Justin nodded and pulled himself to his feet. "You're getting much too big for me to catch." He brushed himself off and eyed her. "Enough horsing around. Mother's waiting."

Andi picked up her schoolbooks and held them close to her chest. "Good-bye, Justin."

"Good-bye." He kissed her forehead then scooped up her hat and plopped it on her head. "Now, get going."

⚜ CHAPTER 3 ⚜

Substitute Teacher

Andi dashed out the front door and slammed it shut. She took the porch steps in one big leap. Two more turns, a zigzag around a big mud puddle, and Andi came to a stop in front of the carriage house. Raindrops splashed her face.

Mother sat in the two-seated buggy, warm and dry under the canvas cover.

"Up you go," Mitch said. He swung Andi into the buggy. "Good-bye, you two. Have fun."

Have fun? Andi made a face and slid onto the buggy seat. It felt strange to ride to school with Mother. Always before Andi rode with Justin and Melinda.

I wish Melinda was here.

If her big sister sat beside her, Andi would not be the only pupil in class with her mother for a teacher. She groaned silently. How many mouths would drop open when they saw Mother ringing the school bell? How many times would Cory poke Andi in the back and snicker?

Nothing like this had happened to Justin when he was a little boy. Or Chad. Or Mitch. Not even to Melinda. Nothing like this had ever happened to Andi either. Not in all of her nine and a half years.

She had never heard of a mother teaching school. Teachers were ladies who never married. Mother was married, even if Father had died four years ago.

Andi sighed. *That's what happens when you have a grown-up brother on the school board.* She slouched against the buggy seat and wished she was curled up in Taffy's stall with a book.

The horse broke into a lively trot. Andi's gloomy thoughts jerked back to the buggy ride. She sat up. Mother was an excellent driver, but the road was rough in places.

The buggy hit a rock and bounced.

Whee! Andi giggled.

"Would you like to drive?"

"Yes, please!" Andi never passed up a chance to take the reins. "Go, Pal!" She slapped the leather reins across the horse's broad back.

Pal trotted faster. Andi wanted to make him

gallop, but Mother shook her head. "It's wet enough without splashing mud into the buggy."

Driving the buggy cheered Andi up. By the time she pulled Pal to a stop in the schoolyard, she was smiling.

When she handed the reins back to Mother, the morning got even better. "When I call your class to come up and recite, I won't ask you any questions," Mother said.

"Really?" Andi's heart gave a happy skip.

How did Mother know Andi didn't want to recite? Her tongue was sure to tie up in knots. She would stutter or give the wrong answer. Mother would be ashamed that her daughter was such a poor pupil.

Mother squeezed Andi's hand. "Yes, really."

Andi squeezed it back. Having Mother for a substitute teacher might not be so bad after all.

Mother backed the buggy under the open shed and took care of Pal while Andi jumped down. Hand in hand, they dodged raindrops, clattered up the steps, and ducked into the schoolhouse.

Andi hung her coat and hat right next to Mother's in the cloakroom.

"It's damp and chilly in here this morning," Mother said. "Would you like to start the fire?"

Andi's eyes grew wide. "Yes, ma'am!" She didn't tell Mother that Miss Hall only let the big boys light the fire.

Wait till that bully Johnny Wilson hears about this!

Andi smiled to herself while she crunched up old newspapers and laid small pieces of kindling in the woodstove. Johnny always boasted about starting the fire for Miss Hall.

He couldn't boast after today.

Andi struck the match. It burst into a tiny blaze, and a sulfur smell exploded in her nostrils. A few seconds later the fire licked up the paper and started right in on the kindling. Soon, the firewood was crackling.

Andi wiped her sooty hands on a rag and closed the stove door. She spread her fingers above the metal top and let the heat chase away the icy feeling in her hands.

That was easy, she thought with satisfaction.

All too soon it was time to ring the bell. Mother stepped out onto the porch. Just before she pulled the rope that would call the children inside, Andi pointed out Johnny Wilson.

"Watch out for Johnny," she whispered. "He's eleven years old and the biggest bully in this town. Maybe in all of California. I don't know what he'll do to a substitute teacher. Probably put molasses on your chair when you're not looking. He's sneaky."

"Thank you for the warning," Mother said. "Now please take your seat."

"Yes, ma'am." Andi hurried back inside and sat down in her empty double seat.

Clang, clang, clang!

Andi's seat didn't stay empty for long. Her friend Rachel slipped in beside her. "Your mother is ringing the—"

"Miss Hall is laid up with that sprained ankle," Andi explained. "The school board asked Mother to take her place until Miss Hall is better." Her heart fluttered. What would her friend say about that?

Rachel didn't say anything.

Cory Blake had plenty to say, though. He plopped down in his seat behind Andi and poked her in the back. "Lucky duck. I wish *my* mother was smart enough to teach school."

"Me too," Rachel echoed with a little sigh.

A warm glow spread through Andi. *They think my mother is smart!*

"Your mothers are both plenty smart," she said generously. "Maybe they can all take turns substitute teaching the next time Miss Hall is sick."

Rachel's smile told Andi she hoped so.

Mother closed the door, walked to the front of the classroom, and picked up a ruler. She rapped it on her desk.

Whispers died down. Every eye turned to stare at the substitute teacher.

Mother smiled. "Good morning, boys and girls.

My name is Mrs. Carter." She stepped to the board and wrote her name in perfect script:

Mrs. Carter

Andi ducked her head. If some of the pupils did not know before who the substitute teacher was, they sure knew now. A dozen pupils gaped at Andi, eyes wide.

Mother dropped the chalk in the tray and turned around. "As you know, Miss Hall had an accident last Tuesday. Dr. Weaver says she must stay off her ankle for some time."

Dead silence.

"The school board asked me to take Miss Hall's place until school lets out for the holidays. I expect you to give me your very best attention and respect during our time together. If you do, we shall all get along splendidly. Do I make myself clear?"

Nobody answered.

"Children?" Mother prompted.

The whole class sat up straight. "Yes, Mrs. Carter."

Mother smiled. "Excellent. Now please stand. We will begin our day by singing 'America.'"

Andi let out a long, grateful breath and stood up with the others.

Mother seemed to know all the school rules. She sang the words to "America" right along with the children. She knew what Bible verses to read. She even knew how to pray out loud in front of the class.

When Andi sat down and opened her reader, she relaxed.

Today was off to a good start.

CHAPTER 4

Bully

Midway through the morning, something hit Andi in the back. Why would Cory bother her? He was her friend.

She ignored him and practiced her spelling words. "Beauty, b-e-a-u-t-y," she whispered. "Broken, b-r-o—"

Splat.

Andi winced. *Not again!* She looked at her seat-mate. Rachel pinched her lips together in disgust and said nothing.

Rachel didn't have to say anything. Andi recognized the giant spitball when it fell from her hair and landed next to her on the seat. *Yuck!*

She whirled on Cory.

Not me, his wide eyes said. He glanced at the teacher then motioned behind his shoulder.

One row over and two rows back, Johnny Wilson was up to his old tricks. He held a large peashooter in one hand. Andi glared at him and mouthed, *Leave me alone!*

He smirked.

A giggle from across the aisle spun Andi around just in time. Mother looked up from helping Mary Ellen. "Quiet, children," she said pleasantly.

Andi went back to her spelling book.

Three spelling words later, something hard and sharp stung Andi's neck. Johnny had gone from shooting nasty spitballs to firing pebbles. He might not be a very good pupil, but that bully was an excellent aim with a slingshot or a peashooter.

Tears of pain and fury watered Andi's eyes. Johnny usually left her alone. But not today. *He wants to make me mad enough to do something to earn a punishment.*

Johnny probably wanted to find out if the substitute teacher would punish her own child.

Andi already knew the answer to that. Mother never played favorites. Andi squeezed her eyes shut and prayed for recess to hurry up and come.

"Jonathan Wilson."

Andi's eyes flew open at the ice in Mother's words. Johnny had better watch out. Mother meant business.

Johnny looked surprised that the substitute teacher knew his name. "Ma'am?"

"The peashooter. In my hand."

Johnny stared at her. So did everyone else. Miss Hall never spoke to her pupils in such a firm, do-it-now-or-else voice. Mother talked like she knew how to handle mischievous boys.

"Now."

Andi squirmed in her seat. What would Mother do if Johnny disobeyed? Would she rap his knuckles with the ruler?

Johnny sprang from his seat as if his britches had caught fire. He tripped, righted himself, and scurried up the aisle. "Yes'm." He handed over the peashooter.

The whole class watched in breathless silence.

Mother carefully examined the weapon. "I have not seen a finer-looking peashooter since Miss Hall gave me the one that belonged to my son Chad." She looked Johnny in the eye. "Do you know what I did with that one?"

Johnny shook his head.

"This." Quick as two gunshots, Mother broke Johnny's weapon into three pieces and dropped them in the trash. "You may return to your studies, Jonathan."

"Yes'm." Red-faced, Johnny crept back to his seat. He opened his spelling book and sat like a stone for the rest of the morning.

Noon recess came, but Andi barely had time to eat. The rain had let up, and Mother was twirling the rope so more girls could jump. Andi stuffed down the rest of her lunch and raced to get in line.

"Miss Hall never turns the rope," Rachel whispered while they waited.

"I know," Andi whispered back. Rain or shine, Miss Hall always stayed indoors.

Andi didn't know what to think. When she ran under the rope, her heart pounded faster than her feet hit the ground.

With Mother turning the rope, Andi made it to sixty-one jumps before she tripped. She skipped to the back of the line and squeezed Rachel's hand. "I beat Mary Ellen by four jumps."

Rachel giggled. "She'll try to make it to a hundred now. You watch and see."

Andi wanted to watch Mary Ellen take her turn, but a movement by the schoolhouse door grabbed her attention. *Johnny!*

What mischief was he up to? Molasses on Mother's chair? A firecracker in the stove? He was probably mad at the substitute teacher for calling him up front. Madder still that she broke his fine peashooter.

Prickles raced up Andi's neck. *I better find out. Mother doesn't know that bully like I do.*

Just then, Johnny jumped off the porch steps and ducked behind the schoolhouse. Before she could chase after him, Mother asked Andi to take her end of the rope. Then she headed toward the schoolhouse.

A minute later, she rang the bell, and the children swarmed inside.

It was too late to do anything about Johnny now. Andi stayed on pins and needles for the next hour. Every time she glanced his way, Johnny was watching Mother. He wore a sneaky smile.

The afternoon crawled by.

When Cory returned to his seat from the blackboard, he was grinning from ear to ear. "Your mother showed me how to work fractions in a way I understand," he told Andi in a low voice. "Now I won't dread arithmetic so much."

Andi forgot about the bully and his tricks. She beamed. *My friends like having Mother for their teacher.*

A scraping noise at the teacher's desk a few minutes later put Andi back on her guard. Mother opened a drawer then stepped back.

Johnny muffled a laugh. Two other boys watched with eager eyes. Even Thomas was smiling.

Mother reached inside the drawer and drew out an enormous bullfrog. Andi caught her breath. Cory gasped. Rachel and two other girls shrieked.

Mother smiled. "Thank you, Jonathan, for sharing this amphibian with us. I believe it's time for a science lesson. Boys and girls, I want you to gather around . . ."

Andi didn't hear the rest. She was too busy laughing with the rest of the class at the look on Johnny's face. If the bully had asked her, Andi could have told him Mother wasn't afraid of frogs. Or of snakes or spiders either.

Mother outsmarted him, she thought. *I guess she knows that bully pretty good, after all.*

Almost before Andi knew it, school was over for the day. Mother dismissed the class. The pupils spilled out of the schoolroom and down the porch steps.

Andi stayed behind. She helped Mother clean the blackboard and straighten the bookshelves. She closed the damper on the stove to make sure the fire went out. When Mother stepped into the cloakroom, Andi opened the drawers in the teacher's desk. She didn't trust Johnny—not one bit.

She finished checking for crawly critters and looked up. Mother was dressed to go. She helped Andi with her coat and hat then held out her hand. "I don't believe we'll have any more trouble with Johnny, do you?"

Andi grinned and took Mother's hand. Johnny would have to think hard to come up with a trick Mother had not already seen from Justin, Chad, or Mitch.

Hand in hand, Andi and Mother stepped through the cloakroom. Mother closed the outer door and locked it. They started down the steps.

"Howdy-do, ma'am."

Mother stopped short. Two men stood at the bottom of the porch steps, blocking their way.

A Mexican with a long, drooping mustache lifted his wide *sombrero* in greeting, *"Buenas tardes,"* he said gruffly.

Mother did not return his afternoon greeting. "You are in our way, gentlemen," she said in her no-nonsense voice. "Please stand aside."

"'Fraid we can't do that," a scruffy-looking man replied. He pulled aside his long, black overcoat. A pistol rested in his holster. "Sorry, ma'am, but you need to come along with Paco and me."

⊰ CHAPTER 5 ⊱

A Big Mistake

At the sight of the pistol, Mother pressed her lips together. A gentle squeeze on Andi's hand warned her not to speak.

Andi could not have talked even if she wanted to. Her tongue was stuck like glue to the roof of her mouth.

"What do you want?" Mother asked coldly.

The scruffy man looked annoyed. "No time for pesky questions." He slid the gun from its holster. "I'll say this as polite as I know how. *Let's go.*"

Andi's stomach turned over. Nobody had ever pointed a gun at her before. She pressed close to Mother's side and buried her head in her mother's warm, woolen coat.

The man chuckled. "Wouldn't want the little girl to get scared now, would we, Miss Hall?"

Miss Hall? Andi choked back a gasp and looked up. *He thinks Mother is Miss Hall?*

A wave of relief washed over Andi. Mother would take care of this big mistake. The man would put away his gun. He'd say he was sorry for mixing up Mother and Miss Hall. He and his Mexican friend would turn around and leave.

But Mother did not take care of it. She put her arm around Andi and looked into the scruffy man's dark eyes. "Let my pupil run along home, and I'll go with you."

No! Andi's thoughts spun. *Don't go with them. Tell them you're not Miss Hall. You are Elizabeth Carter. Please, Mother!*

The man scratched at his dirty beard. "She's just a little gal, but I bet she knows enough to run for the sheriff." He shook his head. "Can't take chances. You're both coming with us."

Andi's heart raced out of control. If Mother would not tell these men who she was, then Andi must. Somebody had to fix this mistake. "She's not—"

A painful squeeze of Andi's hand made her gulp back her words. *Be still*, came the silent command.

The men acted like Andi had not spoken. They waved Mother and Andi down the schoolhouse steps and toward three horses.

Andi counted two men. The third horse must be

for Mother . . . uh . . . Miss Hall. *Why do they want Miss Hall?*

One look at Mother's face kept Andi's question deep inside.

With the gun-toting man's help, Mother mounted the horse. She reached down to help Andi climb up.

Paco, the Mexican man, snatched Andi away. "The little one will ride with me. This way the teacher will do just what we say, *no?*" He tossed Andi on his big, gray horse. Then he swung up behind her. "What is your name?"

Andi obeyed Mother and kept quiet.

"Let her go," Mother ordered. "She will certainly be missed if she doesn't return home soon. You'll have all of Fresno after you." Blue fire flashed from her eyes.

The men didn't look worried. They glanced at each other and shrugged.

"We'll be long gone before anyone knows either of you are missing," Scruffy-face said. He scowled. "Now, tell the kid to answer Paco."

Mother nodded at Andi.

"My name is Andi." Her throat was so dry it came out as a whisper.

"Mucho gusto," Paco replied.

He might be pleased to meet me, but I'm not pleased to meet him, Andi thought. These scruffy men were

bullies, just like Johnny. *No*, she corrected herself. *Worse than Johnny.*

These were grown-up bullies.

Paco jabbed his heels into his horse, and they bounded away.

Andi looked back to see if Mother was really coming. Andi's dark hair blew across her face. When she brushed it away she saw a shadowy figure peeking around the corner of the schoolhouse.

Had a classmate returned to school for a forgotten item? Maybe somebody wanted to ask Mother a question about homework. Whatever the reason, somebody had come back.

Andi twisted her neck farther around to see past Paco's thick middle. The figure stepped out from the shadows. *Cory!*

He nodded at her. Then he slipped behind the schoolhouse and disappeared.

Andi closed her eyes. *Please, Jesus. Send Cory to Justin and the sheriff. Make him hurry!*

Paco yanked her around. "Sit still."

Andi stared between the horse's ears. Everything inside her wanted to scream, "Mother, I'm scared!"

She clamped her teeth together so the words would not slip out. Nobody had to tell Andi that a little girl would not shout "Mother" to an unmarried teacher named Miss Hall.

Andi didn't know why Mother hadn't told the

men she was not Miss Hall. Did she think it was too dangerous, especially when one of them had a gun? Maybe it was better to pretend, at least until Mother could learn what the men wanted.

Andi rubbed her fists in her eyes to smear away sudden tears. She wanted to see if Mother was still coming, but she was afraid to turn around. Paco might yank on her again.

A few minutes later, Scruffy-face and Mother pulled up alongside Paco.

Mother smiled. "You're doing fine, Miss Andrea," she said. "You are one of my bravest pupils. I'm proud of you. Can you be brave a little longer?"

Andi sniffled. "Yes, M—Miss Hall."

Mother nodded. *Keep playing the game*, her eyes warned.

Andi swallowed hard. She didn't know how long she could play along. It would be hard not to slip and say "Mother."

They rode for a long time.

The afternoon sun stayed hidden behind gray clouds.

Rain came and went.

The wind blew cold raindrops into Andi's face. She blinked and shivered.

Andi knew her directions—north, south, east, west. She didn't need to see the sun to know they were heading east. The bare, rolling hills rose higher.

Scrubby-looking oak trees and lots of brush soon covered the hills. Here and there a bristly pine tree rose toward the sky.

The afternoon turned darker, and still they rode. Andi grew saddlesore and hungry.

Worse, Andi needed to find an outhouse. She looked around at the dark shadows. No privy in sight. There were plenty of bushes and trees though. They would work.

But Andi was too scared to tell Paco.

When she couldn't stop wiggling, Paco caught on. He laughed and called to Scruffy-face in Spanish, "The little one is close to having an accident."

Paco made it sound like a big joke. He probably didn't know that Andi could understand his words. Her face blazed in shame.

Scruffy-face yanked his horse to a stop. He jerked his chin at Mother. "See to your pupil's needs." He slid the pistol from his holster. "You both better return real quick . . . *or else.*"

Paco lowered Andi to the ground.

Mother climbed off her horse. She took Andi's hand and led her behind a clump of bushes. "I don't know what they want, sweetheart," she whispered. "But so far they have not hurt us."

"They're bullies," Andi said. "They won't let us go home."

Mother nodded. "I know, but don't be afraid.

Keep pretending I'm Miss Hall. Can you remember to do that?"

Andi nodded. She *had* to remember. What would the men do if they found out they'd made a big mistake? For sure they'd be angry.

Mother said a quick prayer with Andi before they returned to the horses.

Dusk fell. The men urged their horses faster, like they didn't want to be caught outside in the dark.

Andi didn't want to be caught out in the dark either. She heard a creek splashing nearby. Or was it rain hitting the treetops?

She was too tired to figure it out, but the sound of water made her thirsty. She kept quiet about that and yawned. Her eyes closed, and she slumped against Paco.

The next thing Andi knew, Paco was shaking Andi awake.

She opened her eyes. The horse had stopped in the middle of a small clearing. Andi saw a cabin nearly hidden by oak and pine trees. Two yellow squares of light shone out of the windows.

My new home.

⊰ CHAPTER 6 ⊱

Gentleman Outlaw

Paco slid from his horse and lifted Andi down.

After sitting so long on the horse, Andi's legs didn't work. She crumpled to the muddy ground. Her head spun. She was cold and hungry, and very tired. She whimpered.

Mother flew to her side. "Shhh." A finger fell across Andi's lips. "Be brave. Let me help you stand up."

Andi nodded and tried to make her legs obey.

"Here, now." Paco shooed Mother aside. "I'll carry the little one."

The cabin door cracked open. A tall figure blocked the light spilling from inside. "Did you find her?" a deep, rumbly voice asked. "Did everything go as planned?"

Scruffy-face chuckled. "Not exactly."

"What do you mean *not exactly*?"

Scruffy-face pointed to Andi in Paco's arms. "A small snag. The schoolteacher was not alone. We waited till we thought the schoolhouse was empty but . . ." He shrugged.

The shadowy figure stepped off the porch. Frowning, he peered down at Andi. "That's a shame. I don't like surprises."

Andi looked away. *Then let us go home.* She didn't say those words out loud.

"Sorry, boss. There was no way to help it," Scruffy-face said. "We couldn't leave the girl behind. She'd have run straight for the sheriff."

"I reckon you're right." Boss sighed and turned to Mother. A smile replaced his frown. He bowed and offered Mother his arm. "Won't you join me inside, Miss Hall?"

Andi stared. Boss had nice manners—much nicer than the two bullies who had dragged Mother and Andi up here.

Boss also kept himself clean. Up close he smelled like the tonic Andi's brothers used on Sundays to keep their hair slicked down. Boss had neatly combed gray hair and no beard. His shirt was spotless and tucked into his trousers. No buttons were missing.

Compared to Scruffy-face and Paco, Boss looked and talked like a kind old gentleman.

Mother did not return Boss's nice manners. She didn't take his arm. Instead, she edged her way closer to Andi. "I won't join you until I find out why we are here." She lifted her chin. "Do you plan to ransom us?"

"You hear that, Will?" Scruffy-face laughed. "Ransom? You're nothin' but a poor schoolteacher. Who would pay to get you back?"

"Enough, Eli," the boss named Will snapped. "Ma'am." His voice turned gentlemanly again. "Would you please join me inside? It's dark, and the wind and rain are picking up." He offered Mother his arm once more. "Please."

After a long pause, Mother agreed. She refused to take Will's arm though. With her head held high, she crossed the porch and entered the cabin. Her damp skirt swished against the wooden planks.

Paco carried Andi inside. Will followed, limping a little. "Set the girl down and see to the horses. You and Eli have that job tomorrow. Better get plenty of shut-eye."

"*Sí, jefe.*" Paco put Andi down.

As soon as Andi's feet touched the floor, she ran to Mother and threw her arms around her waist. *Oh, Mother, let's get away from here*, she begged silently.

Boss waited until the door thudded shut behind Paco before he spoke. "I am Will—"

"Benton." Mother nodded at his surprised look.

"Yes, Mr. Benton, I know who you are. Your face has stared at me for months from a number of Wanted posters."

"You don't say!" Mr. Benton looked pleased. "I'm famous?"

"For a stagecoach robber," Mother said coldly. "What right do you have to kidnap me and this little girl and drag us up here to the middle of nowhere?"

Andi studied Mr. Benton. He looked ashamed.

"I apologize, ma'am, for bringing you here without asking your permission." He scratched his chin. "But I don't think you would have agreed to come."

"You're right," Mother said.

"I'm also sorry the little girl had to come along. Her family must be upset."

Mother's hold on Andi tightened. "I'm sure they are out of their minds with worry. By now, the sheriff and his men will be searching for us."

"They won't know where to look." Mr. Benton sat down on the fireplace hearth and poked the embers. Sparks flew up. He rubbed his left leg, winced, and looked at Mother. "Nobody has found this place in twenty years. They won't find it now."

Unless Cory saw which direction we rode, Andi thought with hope. Maybe the sheriff was following their tracks right now!

The memory of splashing along a muddy trail

sent an unwelcome lump to Andi's throat. Rain always washed tracks away.

"You will both be safely returned to the valley when you have finished what I brought you here for," Mr. Benton said. "A few weeks. A few months. Depends."

Mother caught her breath. "A few *months*?" She lowered herself into a straight-backed chair and pulled Andi close. "Please tell me, Mr. Benton. Why are we here?"

"The girl is here by accident. You, Miss Hall?" He drew a deep breath. "You are going to teach me to read."

Andi suddenly felt wide awake. Her head snapped up. This old man didn't know how to read? Why, even little Julianna knew how to read. "Mister, how can you not know how to—"

"Hush, Andrea," Mother said. "Forgive my pupil, Mr. Benton. She doesn't mean to be rude. She's hungry and very tired." She glanced around. "Is there anything to eat? And someplace where I can put her to bed?"

Mr. Benton stood up. "Surely, ma'am. I apologize." He limped to the cupboard and pulled out a tin of crackers. He dipped into a bucket to fill a cup with water then carried them to Andi. "Eat up."

Andi gobbled the food without even remembering to say thank you. Mother accepted coffee from Mr. Benton and thanked him for both of them.

When Andi finished her scanty supper, Mr. Benton pointed to a door next to the fireplace. "Through there should suit your needs, ma'am. I didn't figure you'd share it with a young'un, but I expect you'll make do."

Mother stood up. "I expect I will."

She clasped Andi's hand and opened the door. The room was barely large enough to squeeze a narrow bed and a small table inside. The window above the bed held no glass.

Rain and wind blew in through the opening. Andi shivered and wrapped her arms around herself. She couldn't sleep here. The bedcovers were probably damp and cold.

Mother leaned across the bed and pushed a heavy shutter closed. "Better?"

Andi shook her head.

When Mother turned to close the door, Mr. Benton's arm stopped her halfway. "Keep it open, ma'am. It's the only way to heat your room. Wouldn't want the young'un to get cold." He hobbled away.

Mother sighed. Then she pulled back the quilt and felt the bedding. "It's dry, thankfully."

"Moth—"

Her chilly hand covered Andi's mouth. "Not even when we're alone," she whispered. "I don't know what might happen if these men discover I'm not Miss Hall."

"I want to go home," Andi said when Mother removed her hand. "I don't like it here."

"I know." Mother peeled away Andi's wet coat and hat. "You're tired. Things will look brighter in the morning. Mr. Benton may be a stagecoach-robbing scoundrel, but he doesn't appear to be a mean one. I don't think we need to be afraid of him."

Mother helped Andi unbutton her dress and take off her shoes and socks. Then she guided her under the covers. "Remember that I'm here with you, and so is God."

She stroked Andi's hair and kissed her forehead. "Don't ever forget that. Now, say your prayers and go to sleep. I'll sit right here beside you."

"Promise?" Andi strained to see through the half-open doorway. She heard Mr. Benton poking the fire. "What if that man wants you to go back out there? What if he makes you leave me here by myself?"

"I promise I'll stay right here. Close your eyes and go to sleep."

Andi closed her eyes, but she did not fall asleep.

Not for a long, long time.

CHAPTER 7

The Trunk

Andi opened her eyes. The bedroom door stood half open. Light from the big room shone in. She heard Mr. Benton rattling pots and pans and knew it was morning. He was singing a familiar tune. "Oh, give me a home where the buffalo roam . . ."

Did Mr. Benton's cheerful singing mean he would be kind?

No! Andi's mind shouted back. *He might not be the bully the other two are, but he kidnapped us. He's not nice.*

Andi snuggled next to Mother. Right now she felt warm and safe. Their bed was a tight fit, but neither one had fallen out during the night.

Mother's blue eyes opened. "Good morning, sweetheart. How do you feel?"

"Not as scared as I was last night, but . . ." Andi bit her lip. Mother might not tell her, but she had to ask anyway.

"What is it?"

Andi lowered her voice until it was barely a whisper. "Why did you let those men think you're Miss Hall?"

Mother brushed Andi's dark waves away from her face and sighed. "When I saw they were armed, I decided it would be safer to play along."

"They might have let us go if you'd told them they made a mistake."

"I don't think so," Mother said sadly. "At best they would have demanded to know where the real Miss Hall was."

Andi said nothing, so Mother kept whispering. "They might have knocked us out or tied us up and then gone to fetch your teacher. Would you want them to bring Miss Hall here? She would have been terrified."

Miss Hall with her sprained ankle. Andi had not thought about that.

She swallowed. Now she understood why Mother had not told Paco and Eli about the mix-up.

Andi's heart nearly burst with pride in her mother. *If only I can be brave like her*, she thought. *Help me to be brave, God.*

"Mother," Andi whispered, "I just remembered

something. Cory saw us ride off. He probably watched which direction we went. I bet he ran lickety-split to the sheriff's office. Sheriff Tate will tell Justin, Chad, and Mitch. They'll come after us."

"What did I tell you?" Mother smiled. "Things are looking brighter already."

Mr. Benton rapped on the half-open door. "Rise and shine, ladies. Sausage and eggs for breakfast."

Andi sat up and threw back the covers. She smacked her lips. Crackers and water for supper had not been enough to keep her stomach from grumbling. She scooted to the end of the bed and stepped on the floor.

Brrr! Andi wriggled into her school dress as fast as she could. She looked around. "Where are my shoes and socks?"

"Mr. Benton laid them out by the fire so they would be warm for you this morning," Mother said. She had slept in her clothes and was trying to brush the wrinkles out of her skirt. Her long, blond braid hung down her back. She looked as messy as Andi felt.

Andi hurried out into the main room. Sure enough, her shoes and socks lay neatly on the hearth. She pulled them on. *Nice and warm.* She stopped shivering.

Mr. Benton had pulled back the shutters to let in the morning light. It wasn't raining, and the damp,

November air could not reach Andi next to the roaring fire.

"Sit down, Little Miss." Mr. Benton pulled out a chair for her.

He showed Mother her seat and set two tin plates in front of them. They were heaped with sausages and scrambled eggs.

"Got a few hens out back, and that's venison sausage." He smiled. "Made it myself."

Andi ate and ate. This time she said thank you.

Mr. Benton offered Andi coffee with sugar and canned milk, but Mother said no. So Andi drank hot chocolate instead.

Mr. Benton is a real gentleman. Andi relaxed and sipped her cocoa.

After breakfast, Mr. Benton piled the dishes in the wash pan and talked to Mother while he did the cleaning up.

Andi wandered to one of the front windows. She leaned over the window sill and looked outside.

Across the yard, a lean-to housed one horse. Beside it sat a well. Maybe Mr. Benton would let Andi fetch the water. It looked like fun to turn the handle and lower the bucket into the water and then wind it back up.

She turned away from the window. "There's just one horse. Where are the others? And where are those other two men?" She pointed out the window to a small building under the trees. "Do they sleep in that little cabin?"

"Yeah." Mr. Benton turned from clearing off the counter. "Paco and Eli left before sunrise. They've got a job to do."

"What kind of job are they—"

"Speaking of work"—Mr. Benton turned to Mother with eager eyes—"shall we get to it, Miss Hall?"

Mother nodded but said nothing. She sat straight and alert at the table.

Mr. Benton hobbled over to a beat-up trunk sitting against a wall and unlatched it. The top creaked open. Kneeling, he rummaged around inside.

Andi left her place at the window and wandered over. Curiosity made her forget Paco and Eli. What was Mr. Benton up to? She glanced over his shoulder and saw fine dishes, clothing, a leather-bound Bible, and—

Was that a china doll peeking out from under a wad of clothes? Why would Mr. Benton have such a fine doll in his trunk? Before she could ask him, he closed the lid.

"Found it," he grunted. Using the trunk for support, he pushed himself to his feet. He rubbed his leg. "Been a long time since I dug around in that old trunk." He clutched a small, thin book in his hand.

Andi recognized the book at once. It was the

same reader all the Carter children had learned from. *Easy as pie*, she thought.

Mr. Benton held it out to Mother. "I've looked at this book many times, but I can't make sense of it," he said in a halting voice. "I . . . I'd be much obliged if you'd tell me how all the letters go together to make words."

Mother took the reader. "There is no reason to be embarrassed that you cannot read, Mr. Benton," she said graciously. "That is why I'm here, is it not?"

Mr. Benton's clean-shaven cheeks reddened. "Well, I . . ." He cleared his throat. "Yes, ma'am."

Andi looked at Mother in wonder. At this moment she was not Elizabeth Carter, Andi's mother. She was Miss Hall, the schoolmistress. Mr. Benton was a pupil who wanted to learn to read. He was bigger and older than Julianna, but he seemed just as eager to unlock the secrets of the alphabet.

Mother smiled at Mr. Benton and motioned him to join her at the table. When he sat down beside her, she opened the small reader. Andi squeezed in next to Mother and watched.

Mr. Benton frowned at Andi.

"I'll be quiet," she promised.

He grunted.

Andi took his grunt as a yes and glanced down at the book. Someone had scribbled CAᵣOLINE across the inside front cover.

"Who's Caroline?" Andi asked. "Is she your little girl?"

"Andrea," Mother scolded.

Andi clapped a hand over her mouth. She had just broken her promise to keep quiet.

‑ꜟ CHAPTER 8 ꜞ‑

No Place to Go

"**I**'m sorry," Andi said between her fingers.

She held her breath. The last thing she wanted to do was make Mr. Benton angry. Mother had seen his face on a Wanted poster. That made him an outlaw.

Outlaws were dangerous, even ones who acted like gentlemen.

Mr. Benton's face twisted into a smile. "It's all right, Little Miss." He reached across the table and patted Andi's arm. "No harm done."

Andi let out her breath. Her hand dropped to her lap.

"Caroline was my daughter," Mr. Benton explained. "She went away a long time ago." He wrinkled his forehead. "I've lost track of how many years it's been. Her ma up and left one day when Caroline was just a little mite."

He looked around the cabin. "Couldn't take any more of this rough country, I reckon."

Andi followed the man's gaze. "Did Caroline live here?"

"Yes." Mr. Benton held up the reader. "She carried this book around with her all the time. Liked to look at the letters and pictures." He chuckled. "Her ma showed her how to write her name, but Caroline couldn't wait till she was big enough to learn it all."

His eyes turned misty. "Never had the heart to tell her there was no school up here, and my wife didn't know much more than the alphabet."

Andi sat still, but her heart was pounding. *Poor Mr. Benton.* "Where is Caroline now?"

Mr. Benton rubbed his shirt sleeve across his face, and his voice changed. "Enough questions." He shooed Andi away. "It's not raining. Go outside and find something to do. But don't wander off."

Andi jumped up at his grumpy voice. Prickles raced down her neck.

"There's bears and cats in these woods," he added. "They'd be happy to snag you for a quick meal."

"Mr. Benton!" Mother warned. "There is no call to frighten her."

He shrugged. "Sorry, ma'am, but the facts are the facts."

Andi remembered the well. "May I bring in some water?"

At Mr. Benton's nod, Andi slipped on her coat and hat, picked up the bucket next to the hearth, and left. The door thudded shut behind her.

Andi made her way to the well. A wooden bucket was tied to a rope. She turned the crank and watched the bucket go down, down, down until it dropped out of sight.

Splash!

Andi stopped turning. She leaned over and peeked into the dark well. How deep was it? She heard the water but couldn't see it.

Bringing up the full bucket was a different story. It took both hands to turn the handle and haul the heavy load back to the surface. Panting, Andi heaved the bucket over the edge and poured the water into the pail from the cabin.

That was not as much fun as I hoped it would be, Andi thought, catching her breath.

She left the bucket beside the well and wandered between the drippy oak and pine trees that surrounded the clearing. Everywhere she looked she saw trees, scraggly underbrush, and dead grass. Small gullies full of rocks and boulders crisscrossed the woods.

A faraway howl made Andi's heart skip. Mr. Benton said there were cats in these woods. Andi

knew he didn't mean barn cats like Bella and Mouser back on the ranch. He meant mountain lions.

She shivered and headed back to the clearing.

Not far from where Andi came out of the woods, she crossed the trail they had taken to get to this place. Their tracks had been chewed into a dark, muddy mess. Probably Paco's and Eli's tracks from leaving this morning were also mixed up in there.

Would the sheriff and his men ever find them? What if the trail disappeared when it cut through underbrush and grass?

Andi looked around. There was no place to go. The trees all looked alike.

She glanced up at the sky. The sun hid behind a solid mass of gray clouds. The ranch was somewhere to the west, but which way was west?

The trail pointed in the direction they'd come, but it was dark last night. Andi had been asleep when they arrived. For all she knew, the trail wound around and came into camp from a completely different direction.

"I would not know which way to go, even if I ran away," she said. Her voice sounded tiny and alone in the quiet morning. The thought of bears and mountain lions scared her.

She scowled. *Besides, I would never run off and leave Mother.*

Drip, drip, drip. Raindrops splashed Andi's cheeks.

Others hit her forehead. The next moment the sky opened up. Andi dashed to the well, picked up the bucket, and headed for the cabin.

She ducked inside in time to hear Mr. Benton's deep voice reciting the alphabet.

"M, man. N, nose. O—" He broke off and looked at Andi. His brown eyes gleamed. "Listen to this, Little Miss. These letters aren't so hard." He started over. "A, apple . . ."

Andi lugged the bucket to its spot by the fireplace and set it down. Then she pulled off her hat and coat and found a warm spot on the hearth. She sat down to listen.

Mr. Benton recited the entire alphabet. He stumbled over Q and V and X, but he looked pleased with himself anyway.

"That was good," Andi said when he finished. "Maybe you'll learn what you need to by this afternoon. Then we can go home."

A chilly silence fell. Mother's expression told Andi she had said the wrong thing.

Mr. Benton's eyes lost their glow. "Not likely. Learning the alphabet was easy. Learning to string all those letters together will take time."

Andi sighed. Mr. Benton was right about that. "Why do you want to learn to read?" She looked around the room. "I don't see any books."

The grouchy look on Mr. Benton's face softened.

"I'd like to be able to read the signs. Got turned around in the valley a few times because I couldn't make out what the signs were saying. Hardly knew what town I was in."

Andi nodded. That made sense.

Mr. Benton winked at Mother. "Might be fun to read my own Wanted poster someday." He grew quiet. "I've got other reasons too."

"Like what?"

Mr. Benton didn't answer. He rubbed his leg and rose to tend the fire.

Andi took the hint. "What's wrong with your leg?" she asked instead.

He chuckled. "You got more curiosity than ten cats. Just like my Caroline. Questions morning, noon, and night. She could talk the hind leg off a mule . . ."

His voice trailed off. He grabbed a poker and stirred the fire.

Andi glanced at Mother, who pressed her lips together and shook her head. *Let him be,* her look said.

"Fetch me a couple chunks of wood, will you, Little Miss?"

Andi jumped to obey.

After Mr. Benton added the logs to the fire, he told Andi, "That's what I always called Caroline: Little Miss." He smiled in fond memory. Then he hiked his left leg up on the hearth and rolled up his trouser leg.

A long, wrinkled wound ran from his boot top to just above his knee. It was an ugly scar, still red and swollen. "Got this a couple weeks ago when we held up a coach along the Yosemite stage line."

Andi stared. It looked like a deep cut from a sword or a long knife.

Mr. Benton traced his finger along the scar. "Got away with plenty of loot, but I also took along this souvenir. It won't heal proper."

For a moment, Andi forgot Mr. Benton was an outlaw. He missed his little girl and called Andi by Caroline's pet name. He was polite and wanted to learn to read. He had a painful wound. He sometimes looked sad.

Andi laid her hand over Mr. Benton's large, rough one. "I'm sorry."

She really was sorry. And strange as it seemed, she was beginning to like this gentleman outlaw.

⇥ CHAPTER 9 ⇤

The Letter

It rained so hard the next three days that Mr. Benton would not let Andi outdoors except to use the privy. He wouldn't let her go to the well but fetched the water himself, hobbling there and back on his bad leg.

When Andi protested, he snapped, "It wouldn't do me any good if you caught pneumonia way up here."

Andi was strong and healthy. She had no intention of catching a cold, much less pneumonia. She told him so. Mother did too.

Mr. Benton stood firm. "My house, my rules, ma'am."

Andi spent most of her time shuffling from window to window, staring outside and wishing she was home. She missed Taffy and wondered who was taking care of her. Andi missed her brothers too . . . almost as much as she missed Melinda in far-off San Francisco.

All day long Andi listened to Mr. Benton drone on and on. He read sentences like, "The man has a hat. The lad has a cap."

It was the dreariest way Andi could think of to spend a rainy day.

Just before lunchtime on the fourth day, Mr. Benton suddenly stopped reading. He put down his book, clomped over to the old trunk, and threw open the lid. "Take a look inside, Little Miss. Maybe you can find something to amuse yourself."

Andi wanted to hug Mr. Benton. "Thank you!" She knelt beside the trunk. What wonders might she find inside?

Andi itched to get her hands on that china doll she'd seen the other day. She pushed aside little girl's dresses and a cigar box full of jewelry and gently lifted the doll into the light.

Everyone on the Circle C ranch knew that Andi would rather play with Taffy than with dolls and tea parties. But on this gloomy morning Andi was desperate. She admitted silently that the doll was beautiful. A real treasure.

Andi stroked the doll's yellow curls. "Did she belong to Caroline?"

Mr. Benton nodded. "I planned to give her that doll on her fifth birthday but . . . well . . . she and her ma were gone by then." He cleared his throat. "You can play with her if you like."

The cabin door flew open just then. Eli and Paco clattered inside, sopping wet.

Paco kicked the door shut. "Look, *jefe*."

Eli dropped two bulging sacks on the table. "The Millerton stage never knew what hit them."

The two highwaymen threw off their soaking ponchos. Water splashed across the floor. They helped themselves to the pot of bubbling stew over the fire.

While they ate, Eli started in on the details of their holdup.

Mr. Benton stopped him cold. "Not in front of the ladies. Finish your stew and take the loot out to the shack. I'll come by later to hear the whole story and divide it up."

Andi turned back to the trunk. She didn't want to look at the two outlaws. Mr. Benton was polite, but she did not like Paco and Eli. *Bullies!* Her shaking fingers dug deeper inside the trunk.

The men scraped their plates clean and rose.

Andi's stomach rumbled. *I wonder if they left anything for us.*

"Did anybody come after you?" Worry crept into Mr. Benton's voice.

"No one, *jefe*," Paco told him.

"Our tracks washed out as quick as we made them," Eli said, picking up the sacks.

The two men left, slamming the door behind them.

Quiet fell, and Andi relaxed.

"I apologize for their roughness, ma'am," Mr. Benton said. "This bum leg of mine won't let me join my partners. Figured it would be a good time to learn to read. Sure can't do much else till my leg heals."

"And that prompted you to steal my pupil and me?" Mother demanded. The sight of Mr. Benton's two companions had clearly stirred up her anger. "Because it was handy for you?"

"Yep." Mr. Benton laughed. "By spring this injury will be no more than a bad memory." He rubbed his leg and winked at Mother. "By then I'll most likely have learned enough to read the Good Book from cover to cover."

Andi said nothing, but she was thinking a lot. It would be good if Mr. Benton could read the Bible. Maybe he'd see the commandment about not stealing. He was pretty nice for an outlaw, but he needed to learn a whole lot about right and wrong.

She smiled to herself and brushed her fingers against a packet of folded papers at the bottom of the trunk. Curious, she lifted them out. She untied the string and let the papers fall to her lap. Letters?

Andi's heart beat faster when a photograph fell out from between the papers. She picked it up. The portrait of a young woman about Justin's or Chad's age looked back at her. *Is this Caroline all grown up? Or is this Caroline's mother?*

At the table, Mr. Benton was reading to Mother. He didn't pay any attention to Andi.

She unfolded one of the letters and read in a whisper, "Dear Papa, I hope this letter finds you well. It has taken me a long time to learn where to send it. I trust this one has made—"

Andi spun around. "Mr. Benton, are these letters from Caroline?" She held up the photograph. "Is this her likeness?"

Mr. Benton jumped up from his chair. It fell backward and crashed to the floor. He hobbled across the room and lunged for the letters. "Those are none of your business!" he shouted.

Andi dropped the letters and leaped away from the angry man. She ran shaking to Mother. The letters lay scattered all over the floor.

"Mr. Benton!" Mother pulled Andi into a tight hug.

Mr. Benton took a deep breath and scooped up the letters. "You are just a mite too curious, Little Miss," he said in a quieter voice.

He sighed. "Didn't mean to scare you. I apologize." He looked ashamed of himself. "Yes, it's my

Caroline all grown up. She's been writing to me since last summer."

Cheered by his willingness to say he was sorry, Andi untangled herself from Mother. "Is that why you want to learn to read? So you can read Caroline's letters yourself?"

He nodded.

Poor Mr. Benton. He had his daughter's letters, but he couldn't read them. It probably drove him crazy. How could he ask just anyone to read such personal letters out loud?

Mr. Benton dropped the letters into the trunk and banged it shut. Then he stomped outside and slammed the door.

Andi returned to the trunk. Sniffing back tears, she picked up the china doll and sat down on the lid. "I want to go home."

"We will, Andrea," Mother said from her seat at the table. "Be brave for now."

Andi smoothed the doll's skirt and looked down. One of the letters caught her eye. It had not made it back inside the trunk. A sudden thought made her smile.

Maybe Mr. Benton would like me to read him a letter sometime. It would almost be like Caroline reading it. He might like that.

She picked up the paper and unfolded it.

Andi's heart thumped like a galloping horse the

moment she started reading. This letter was not from Caroline. Instead, the words seemed to come straight out of one of Mitch's dime novels.

But this adventure story was real: A dying outlaw. Stolen gold. Hidden treasure. The outlaw was giving Mr. Benton his loot for saving his life many years ago.

No wonder Mr. Benton wanted to learn to read for himself! Not just to hear from Caroline. This letter was a treasure map in words. Andi shivered. "Mother, listen to—"

The door swung open. Mr. Benton limped inside with a load of wood. He dumped it in the woodbox, brushed his hands together, and said, "It's lunchtime, Miss Hall. Then back to my lessons."

Andi folded the letter and stuffed it in her dress pocket.

☆ CHAPTER 10 ☆

Into the Woods

"**A**ndrea."

Mother's voice crept into Andi's dreams and woke her up with a start. It was very early. No light peeked into the room through the half-open doorway. No pans rattled.

"Sweetheart, I need you to be the bravest you have ever been," Mother whispered.

Andi sat up, wide awake. "Why? What happened?"

"Nothing yet, but it's been five days. If we are not found soon, it will turn too cold to keep up the search. I don't know how high we are, but it feels cold enough to snow."

"Snow?"

Andi had never seen snow. When her brothers cut a tree each Christmas, they came back from the mountains with stories of the cold, white blanket that sparkled in the sun and covered everything.

"I'd like to see snow," she whispered.

"Perhaps someday. But today you must make your way down to the lowlands and find help. A sheepherder's hut. A ranch. Anything."

Andi gasped. "By *myself*?" A cold lump settled in her belly. She shook her head. "I don't want to leave you."

Mother gripped Andi's shoulders. "You will obey me in this, Andrea. Last night, Eli and Paco joined Mr. Benton for a fireside chat. I'm sure they thought I was asleep."

A scraping noise made Mother flinch. She and Andi sat quiet as two mice.

"Mr. Benton told his men they needed to pick up winter supplies," Mother said when no other noises followed. "Eli asked how long 'this school foolishness' was going to last. It sounds like Mr. Benton plans to keep us here until he can read well, maybe even through the winter."

No! Andi squeezed her eyes shut so Mother wouldn't see the tears swimming up.

Mother busied herself helping Andi dress. She buttoned Andi's shoes and whispered instructions. "I heard a creek the evening they brought us up here. Find it and follow it."

Andi stood stiff and scared and didn't answer.

Her heart hammered. Her fingers and toes felt numb. *Maybe this is just a horrible nightmare.*

Mother gently shook her. "Andrea. Pay attention."

Andi opened her eyes.

Mother's face was pale, but her words came out strong and steady. "I found Mr. Benton's hunting knife. He probably won't miss it until you're far away. Use it to cut into the bark on trees and mark your way. Or cut branches and pile them. Something so you can find your way back with the sheriff."

"Which way do I go?" Andi's voice shook.

"Downhill. Then follow the creek." Mother pushed Andi's arms into her coat and adjusted her hat. "It's not as far away as you might think."

She climbed up on the bed and drew back the shutter. It opened without creaking. "At least it's not raining."

"You come too," Andi begged.

Mother shook her head. "Mr. Benton would discover right away that we left. He'd send Eli and Paco after us. They have guns. I will keep Mr. Benton busy all morning. I'll tell him you aren't feeling well. He won't disturb you, not if I insist you be left alone."

She smiled. "Outlaw he may be, but Mr. Benton is a gentleman."

Andi looked at the window then back at Mother. Andi blinked back tears but a couple leaked out.

Mother pulled her into a tight hug. "I am

counting on you to rescue me." She kissed Andi's forehead. "You can do this. God will go with you."

Andi rubbed away her tears with the back of her hand. She nodded.

"Good girl," Mother said. "Here's the knife."

Thankfully, it was in a sheath. Andi slipped it into her large coat pocket.

Mother held out a tied bandana. "Here's a little food I found in the middle of the night. Eat slowly. It will take all morning—maybe longer—to walk out of these hills. Don't give up. When you come across a hut or a ranch house, tell whoever lives there what you did to mark the trail."

She kissed Andi again and lifted her up to the window sill.

Holding tightly to Andi's hands, Mother prayed, "Protect her, Lord, and show her the way."

Then she lowered Andi to the ground. "Now go, sweetheart. Take the trail. It disappears soon, but it will start you in the right direction." She dropped the bandana.

Andi caught it and looked up. "Mother, I—"

Mother blew her a kiss and closed the shutter with a soft *thud*.

Andi stood trembling beneath the window. The chilly, gray morning promised another day of rain. She pulled her hat down farther over her ears. She didn't know which way was north, south, east, or west, but Mother said the trail went in the right direction.

Andi took a deep breath and darted around the corner of the cabin. The yard was empty. Three horses stood under the lean-to. She crept past, hoping she wouldn't startle them.

The horses didn't make a sound.

When Andi reached the trail, she let out her breath and broke into a run. *Run fast. Run far away!* In no time, her shoes were caked with thick, sloppy mud.

After ten minutes of running, the trail opened up into an oak meadow. Andi stopped and looked around. She panted to catch her breath. "Which way now?" she asked.

Nobody answered. Not even a bird was up this early. Probably they'd all flown south for the winter. *I wish I could fly*, Andi thought with a sigh. *I'd fly clear over these trees.*

"Downhill. Then follow the creek." Mother's instructions whispered in Andi's mind.

She turned toward the part of the clearing that sloped downward and jogged across the soggy, dead grass. Soon she was walking between scraggly oak trees growing close together. The underbrush reached out and snagged her coat.

"The knife!" Panic set in. She'd almost forgotten to mark her trail.

Andi chose a tree, unsheathed the knife, and began to dig. The bark was rough, with too many grooves. She hacked and hacked, but her hard work barely left a dent.

She stuffed the knife back in her pocket and looked around for dead wood. It was much easier to pile branches in the shape of a big X than to cut into a tree trunk. When Andi had finished, she backed up. The X was easy to see on top of the short, dead grass in the clearing.

She let out a sigh of relief and kept going.

The gloomy woods brightened as the sun rose. Her terror at leaving Mother and traveling through this wild place lessened.

So far, nothing bad had happened. No one was chasing her. It wasn't raining. The land went steadily downhill. She left piles of dead branches behind her.

Andi smiled. Maybe Mother was right. *I can do this!*

Sometime later, Andi's belly told her it was long past breakfast time. She stopped and opened the bandana. Two biscuits and a chunk of cheese stared up at her. She made a face. Not much of a breakfast.

Andi gobbled up one biscuit and half the cheese. She carefully wrapped up the rest and slipped the bandana into her other pocket.

It was harder to run now. Andi picked her way around the scratchy underbrush that blocked her way. An easier-looking path went to the left, but it did not go downhill. No matter how rough the path was, Andi knew she must always go downhill.

The wind picked up. Rain began to fall. Andi ducked under a tree. Her shoe caught on a root and down she went.

Ouch! Andi sat up and rubbed her knees. Then she heard a rushing noise.

"Follow the creek."

Andi smiled. She was going in the right direction. She stood up and headed for the water.

CHAPTER 11

Follow the Creek

Andi looked down. She clasped her hands and wondered what to do. Following the creek would not be easy.

Rushing below her in a shallow, rocky gully, the creek flowed downward. Bushes stuck out from the banks. Boulders and dead wood lined the sides. Up here, where Andi was safe from the noisy stream, trees grew thick along the bank. She would have to walk a long way around to find a clear path.

What if I walk too far and lose the creek?

Mother's words came back. *"Follow the creek."*

Scared or not, Andi had to obey. She spent a long time gathering dead branches. She used the knife to cut bushes and add them to the wood. "I'll make this pile so big that nobody can miss it," she yelled at the creek.

The sheriff would know just where to leave the watery path when he came back this way.

Step by careful step, Andi worked her way to the bottom of the gully.

Branches slapped her face. They grabbed her coat and wouldn't let go. She yanked her sleeve from a thorn bush and stepped down farther.

A narrow path ran alongside the creek. Andi followed it for what seemed like hours. "I wonder what animals use this path."

For sure she did not want to meet a wild animal face-to-face. Even a harmless beaver sounded scary with the cold, swift water tumbling beside her.

"Hurry, hurry!" the creek seemed to be shouting at her.

Andi hurried, but not too fast. The rocks were slippery. She held on to branches to keep her balance. The cold, drizzly rain chilled Andi to the bone. Her woolen coat didn't feel warm anymore.

The animal path disappeared. Not far away, the splashing grew louder. The ground dropped, and a small waterfall tumbled over the rocks.

Andi didn't stop to admire the pretty falls. Shivering, she picked her way downstream.

Snap! Something big and brown tore through the underbrush.

Andi shrieked, slipped, and fell on the rocks. One leg landed in the creek. She picked herself up and stumbled away. Water dripped from her coat.

"Please, God," she cried, "take care of me. Please, no mountain lions." She wrapped her arms around herself and hid in the bushes.

A deer bounded across the creek and crashed through the trees on the other side. Andi's heart slowed, but she couldn't stop shaking. She came out of hiding and continued on her way.

What a horrible day! Her throat felt tight with tears. *I want Mother!*

"Be brave," Mother's voice whispered in Andi's head.

The rain suddenly stopped. White, feathery flecks began to fall.

Andi stopped short. Snow? The flakes fell into the creek and vanished. They landed on the rocks and melted.

Dozens of flakes stuck to Andi's red coat. *It's snow.* She looked up. Bits of white stung her cheeks. Smiling, she brushed them away. *I've seen snow!*

Soon the snow changed back to a drizzly rain. Andi's teeth chattered. She stuffed her icy hands under her armpits and trudged on.

Andi's coat and hat were soaked now. Her feet felt like two ice chips. She was hungry, but the remaining biscuit had crumbled into a drippy mess. The cheese was slimy. She threw it away, bandana and all.

"I c-can't give up," she stammered. "Mother is counting on me." She kept putting one foot in front of the other.

What felt like hours later, the creek began to widen out. Loud splashing turned to a low gurgling. It wasn't flowing downhill as quickly as it had before, and the trees stood farther apart.

The creek soon flowed into a large clearing. Andi moved away from the water, away from the slippery rocks and squishy mud. She looked around for a sheepherder's hut. Maybe a few sheep were grazing in the rain.

She didn't see any sheep or huts, but four riders were watering their horses at the creek.

Andi took off running toward the group. "Help!" she hollered. "I need—"

Thunk!

Andi tripped over a grassy mound and fell flat on her face. She tried to stand up, but she was too dizzy. She crumpled back to the ground. "Help!"

Andi glanced up. The men were too far away to hear her shouts.

Suddenly, the riders galloped toward her. And just a minute later, Justin was lifting Andi into his arms. "Hurry," he said, "she's dripping wet and shaking with cold."

Mitch yanked off his rain poncho. Then he took off his jacket and handed it to Justin. His blue eyes were wide with worry. "You all right, Andi?"

Andi shook her head. "I'm c-cold."

"Where have you been?" Sheriff Tate asked.

"The questions can wait," Chad said. He helped Justin pull off Andi's wet coat and wrap her in Mitch's warm, dry jacket.

Justin draped Mitch's poncho over Andi to keep off the rain. "We need to find shelter and build a fire." He rubbed Andi's back then pulled her close.

"No!" Andi squirmed. "We have to go back for Mother."

"Take it easy," Mitch said. He didn't seem to mind the rain soaking his shirt and trousers.

"A stagecoach robber named Will Benton has her," Andi said. "We have to go back before it gets too dark to follow the trail."

Sheriff Tate's eyebrows shot up. "Will Benton? What does he want with you and your mother?"

Through chattering teeth, Andi explained everything that had happened. "Mr. Benton planned to keep us all winter," she finished. "That's why Mother sent me out the window to find help."

She tugged on Justin's rain gear. "When he finds out Mother helped me run away, he'll know I'm bringing back help. He'll take Mother and go deeper into the mountains. Please, Justin. Go get her. Before it's too late."

"We have no idea where they're holed up." Sheriff Tate sounded exhausted. "We've been searching these hills for nearly a week. There's no sign of them for a hundred miles."

Andi snuggled closer to Justin. "They're good hiders, but not good enough." She smiled. "I can show you the way there."

⊰ CHAPTER 12 ⊱

Outlaw Friend

Sheriff Tate shook his head. "In this downpour? No. You need dry clothes and—"

"She'll be fine," Chad cut in. "We're not leaving our mother out there one more night. Andi's our best chance of finding her."

"Please, Sheriff," Andi pleaded. "I can do this. I'll stay warm in Mitch's jacket and poncho."

Sheriff Tate mounted his horse. "You Carters are a stubborn bunch," he mumbled. "Don't blame me if Andi comes down with pneumonia from tramping around the wilderness in this weather."

Justin mounted Thunder and settled Andi in front of him. "Are you sure you're up to this, honey?"

"Yes." She clenched her jaw so Justin couldn't see her chattering teeth. She pointed to the creek. "That way."

Following the creek on horseback felt like heaven compared to Andi's earlier trek. The horses' hooves clattered over rocks in the rushing stream. When the gully grew steeper, the men urged their mounts up the bank and kept going.

Unlike a little girl on foot, the sheriff and Andi's brothers didn't need to stay right next to the creek. They trotted around the underbrush and scraggly trees. An hour later they found the creek again. How could they do that?

Andi wanted to ask, but she was too cold and too tired. She pinched herself to stay awake. When the horses neared the creek for a third time, she kept her eyes on the ground. There was something familiar about this place.

Where did I enter the creek? "There!" She pointed. Nobody could miss her biggest pile.

Justin squeezed Andi's shoulder. "Good job."

It was harder to find the piles of dead wood Andi had shaped like X's. The horses crisscrossed the oak forest while she looked for the other markers. Back and forth. Back and forth. How many piles had she made on her way to the creek?

Andi couldn't remember.

On and on they went. Another hour passed. "The trail should be here somewhere," Andi said. She choked back a sob. "I can't find it!"

"Easy, honey," Justin said. "You're doing fine."

A few minutes later, Mitch waved them over. Sure enough, a faint trail wound its way through the oaks.

Everyone dismounted. Justin settled Andi under a tree and tightened his gun belt around his hips. "How far is it to the cabin?" he asked her.

"I don't know. Not too far." She eyed her brother's pistol. "Please don't shoot anybody."

"We might not have a choice," Justin said. "The sheriff wants to capture Will Benton and his men alive, but if they resist . . ." He smiled. "It's not your worry."

It is too my worry! What if Mother got caught in the crossfire?

Andi clamped her jaw shut to keep her words inside. She watched her brothers. They had moved away and were deep in a hushed conversation with Sheriff Tate.

They don't want me to hear their plans to shoot Mr. Benton, she thought. *I have to warn Mother to hide before it's too late.*

Andi didn't want to think about how much trouble she might get into. She didn't want to think about how dangerous it was. She yanked Mitch's poncho over her head, wriggled out of his heavy jacket, and sprang to her feet.

Without a backward glance, she darted down the trail.

"Andi!"

She ignored her brothers and kept running.

The clearing was farther away than Andi remembered. She ran until she couldn't breathe. Finally, she broke into the clearing . . . and stopped short.

Paco and Eli stood between her and the cabin.

"Where have you been all day?" Eli grabbed Andi before she could run. "Did you plan to bring back help but got lost in the woods instead?"

"Let me go, you bully!" Andi shrieked.

Eli laughed. "Silly little girl. You look like a drowned rat." He opened the cabin door and dragged Andi inside. "Found her, boss. She must have walked around in circles all day. Lucky no mountain lion got her."

Paco hurried inside behind Eli and shut the door.

"Andrea!" Mother's face turned pale.

"That was a fool thing to try, Little Miss," Mr. Benton said. "But I'm glad you had the sense to come back." He smiled his relief. "You must be hungry."

Andi fell into her mother's arms. She was too scared to be hungry. "I'm sorry, Mother. I—"

Mother clapped her hand over Andi's mouth and drew her close to the fire. "Shhh. Let's get you dried off."

Crash! Mr. Benton's chair hit the floor. He rose to his full height. *"Mother?"* He stared at her. "What's going on here? You're the schoolteacher. You're Miss Hall."

Andi froze in horror. She'd forgotten her instructions and had now put Mother in danger.

Silence fell over the group. Nobody moved. The fire snapped and crackled.

"This is Chad Carter!" Chad's angry shout tore through the quiet room. "You are surrounded. Send out my mother and sister, and the sheriff promises there will be no gunfire."

Mr. Benton's mouth dropped open. "Carter? You're *Elizabeth Carter*?" He hobbled across the room and grabbed his pistol from the mantel above the fireplace. "The Circle C ranch?"

Mother nodded. "I took Miss Hall's place in the classroom for—"

"Enough!" Mr. Benton roared.

Andi shook all over. Her eyes were glued on the gun in Mr. Benton's hand. Would he shoot them? She pressed closer to Mother.

"Well, that's just *great*. I told you the plan was too risky." Eli pulled out his pistol. "This isn't over, boss."

"It is for me," Paco said in Spanish. "I'm not going up against the Carters *and* the sheriff. I'm getting out of here." He slipped into the tiny bedroom.

A minute later Andi heard an *oof*, and then a yelp.

"One down," Mitch yelled.

With the speed of a striking rattlesnake, Eli yanked Andi away from Mother.

Andi screamed and kicked.

"No, Eli!" Mr. Benton ordered.

"I'm not getting caught like a rat in a trap." He hiked Andi up under one arm and threw the door wide open. "Let me ride out of here," he yelled, "and I'll leave the girl on the trail." He took a step onto the porch. "What do you say?"

Andi thrashed and yelled. Eli hung on tighter. "Carter? You hear me?"

"Be still, Andrea," Mother called. "Everything will be all right."

Andi obeyed and went limp. She turned her head to look back at Mother.

Step by quiet step, Mr. Benton was crossing the room. A heartbeat later he came up behind Eli and shoved his pistol into the scruffy man's back. "Nice and easy, Eli. Drop your six-shooter."

Thud! Eli's gun dropped to the porch.

The next instant Mother snatched Andi and flew off the porch. Justin appeared and rushed to meet them. Andi threw her arms around his neck.

Chad, Mitch, and Sheriff Tate raced past them and surrounded the men, guns drawn.

"It's over, boys," the sheriff growled.

⚔ ⚔

"Are those things really necessary?" Mother was frowning at the handcuffs circling Mr. Benton's wrists. "I told you how decently he treated us, and you saw how he saved Andrea."

Sheriff Tate finished tying the three captured outlaws to their saddle horns. "Tell it to the judge, Elizabeth. I'm just doing my job."

"I'm sorry for all the trouble, ma'am," Mr. Benton said from the back of his horse. "Never meant for you or the little miss to get hurt or scared. I just wanted to read Caroline's letters."

"And this letter too?" Andi pulled the soggy paper from her dress pocket and unfolded it. The ink had smeared until the words were unreadable. "The one from the dying outlaw? About the gold he left you? I found it on the floor."

Mr. Benton's eyes nearly popped out of his head. "Do you know where the gold is?"

Andi shook her head.

Mr. Benton's breath came out like a leaky balloon. "I reckon it wasn't meant to be." He gave Andi a lopsided smile. "No hard feelings?"

Andi shook her head. Sadness squeezed her heart. Mr. Benton had saved her from Eli. He'd acted like a grandfather toward her. It was too bad he had to go to jail.

But maybe . . .

Andi ran back inside the cabin. She heaved open the trunk's lid and took out Caroline's letters. Then she hurried back outside. "I have an idea." She reached up and stuffed the letters into Mr. Benton's pocket. "Mother could come by the jail every day after school and teach you to read."

Mother smiled her agreement.

"And I'll come along and read Caroline's letters to you." Andi smiled up at the old man.

The gentleman outlaw's eyes turned misty. "I would like that very much, Little Miss."

A few minutes later the family mounted up. Mother looked cramped and wet riding with Mitch, but Andi was too happy to be going home to care about the rain. She leaned back against Justin and whispered, "Thank you for coming after us."

"You have someone else to thank too, you know," Justin said.

Andi twisted around to look at him. "Who?"

"Cory told the sheriff what happened. He also watched which direction you and Mother went."

Good ol' Cory! Andi couldn't wait to get back. She would give him a chance to win back his special aggie marbles.

Better yet, she'd *give* the aggies back to Cory as thanks.

History Fun
Black Bart, a Gentleman Outlaw

When people see the word *outlaw*, they usually picture a criminal who robs banks, shoots people, and breaks the law. Most of the outlaws in the Old West fell into that group. They created fear and destroyed people's lives when they broke the law.

Once in a while, however, a different kind of outlaw appeared. The character of Will Benton is a little bit like the real-life outlaw Black Bart (Charles E. Boles). He began his stagecoach robbing career in California in 1875, two years before Andi's adventure in this story.

Black Bart's first robbery was a Wells Fargo stage-coach. He stepped out in front of the stage, raised his shotgun, and politely said, "Please throw down the box." It looked like six other robbers were surrounding the stagecoach, hiding behind boulders with their rifles. However, when Black Bart left with the money box, the passengers saw the rifles were really sticks.

Black Bart was a gentleman outlaw. He demanded the money box from the stage, but he never robbed the passengers, fired a shot, or hurt anyone. He was especially polite to women. When he was finally caught, lawmen discovered that his shotgun was not even loaded! He twice left poetry at the scene of his crimes, which added to the mystery of this strange outlaw.

Sometimes months went by when Black Bart didn't rob at all. When he did, Bart always picked a spot in the mountains where the stagecoach had to slow down.

In 1883, after robbing Wells Fargo stagecoaches twenty-eight times and getting away with $18,000 in his eight-year career, Black Bart's luck ran out. He was shot in the hand and caught. He went to prison, served his time, and was released early.

Then he walked away and disappeared without a trace.

**For more Andi fun,
download free activity pages
at CircleCSteppingStones.com.**

Susan K. Marlow is always on the lookout for a new story, whether she's writing books, teaching writing workshops, or sharing what she's learned as a homeschooling mom. Susan is the author of several series set in the Old West—ranging from new reader to young adult—and she enjoys relaxing on her fourteen-acre homestead in the great state of Washington. Connect with the author at CircleCSteppingStones.com or by emailing Susan at SusanKMarlow@kregel.com.

Leslie Gammelgaard, illustrator of the Circle C Beginnings and Circle C Stepping Stones series, lives in beautiful Washington state where every season delights the senses. Along with illustrating books, Leslie inspires little people (especially her four grandchildren) to explore and express their creative nature through art and writing.

Grow Up with Andi!

Don't miss any of Andi's adventures in the
Circle C Beginnings series

Andi's Pony Trouble
Andi's Indian Summer
Andi's Fair Surprise
Andi's Scary School Days
Andi's Lonely Little Foal
Andi's Circle C Christmas

Visit AndiandTaffy.com
for free coloring pages,
learning activities, and more!

For readers ages 9–13!

**Andi's adventures continue in
the Circle C Adventures series**

*Andrea Carter and the Long Ride Home
Andrea Carter and the Dangerous Decision
Andrea Carter and the Family Secret
Andrea Carter and the San Francisco Smugglers
Andrea Carter and the Trouble with Treasure
Andrea Carter and the Price of Truth*

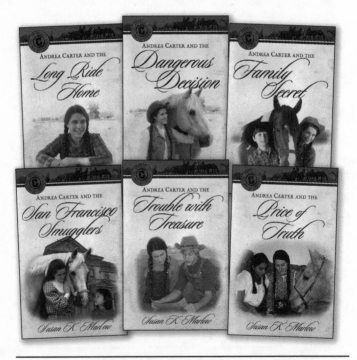

**Free enrichment activities are available at
CircleCAdventures.com.**